Lodusky

Frances Hodgson Burnett

Contents

LODUSKY

BY

Frances Hodgson Burnett

LODUSKY
By Frances Hodgson Burnett

They were rather an incongruous element amid the festivities, but they bore themselves very well, notwithstanding, and seemed to be sufficiently interested. The elder of the two--a tall, slender, middle-aged woman, with a somewhat severe, though delicate face--sat quietly apart, looking on at the rough dances and games with a keen relish of their primitive uncouthness; but the younger, a slight, alert creature, moved here and there, her large, changeable eyes looking larger through their glow of excitement.

"Thet gal thar," drawled a tall mountaineer who supported himself against the chimney and spat with placid regularity into the fire. "They tell me thet gal thar hes writ things as hes been in print. They say she's powerful smart--arns her livin' by it. 'T least thet's what Jake Harney says, 'n they's a-boardin' at Harney's. The old woman's some of her kin, 'n' goes 'long with her when she travels 'round."

There was one fiddler at work sawing industriously at one tune which did good service throughout the entertainment; there was a little furious and erratic reel-dancing, and much loud laughter, and good-natured, even if somewhat personal, jest. The room was one of two which formed the house; the walls were of log; the lights the cheery yellow flare of great pine-knots flung one after the other upon the embers.

"I am glad I thought of North Carolina," Rebecca Noble said to herself. "There is a strong hint of Rembrandt in this,--the bright yellow light, the uncouth figures. Ah! who is that?"

A short time after, she made her way through the crowd to her relative's corner among the shadows. She looked eager and excited, and spoke in a quick, breathless fashion.

"I want to show you something, if you have not already seen it," she said. "There is in this room, Aunt Miriam, the most wonderful creature your eyes ever rested on! You must prepare yourself to be startled. Look toward the door--at that tall girl standing with her hands behind her."

She was attired in a calico of flaunting pattern, and leaned against the log wall in an indifferent attitude, regarding the company from under the heavy lashes of her eyes, which had a look of stillness in them which was yet not repose. There was something even secretive in her expression, as if she watched them furtively for reasons of her own. At her side stood a big, discontented-looking young man, who confronted aggressively two or three other young men equally big, if not equally discontented, who seemed to be arguing some point with him and endeavoring to engage the attention of his companion. The girl, however, simply responded to their appeals with an occasional smile, ambiguous, if not scornful.

"How I wish I could hear them!" exclaimed Miss Noble.

It was her habit to utilize any material she chanced to find, and she had really made her summer jaunt to North Carolina in search of material, but she was not thinking of utilizing this girl, as she managed to keep near her during the remainder of the evening. She had merely found something to be keenly interested in, her interest in any human novelty being, on occasion, intense. In this case her interest increased instead of diminished. She found the girl comporting herself in her natural position as belle, with a calm which was slightly suggestive of "the noble savage." Each admirer seemed to be treated with indifference alike, though there were some who, for reasons best known to themselves, evidently felt that they stood more securely than the rest. She moved through game and dance with a slow yet free grace; she spoke seldom, and in a low, bell-like monotone, containing no hint of any possible emotional development, and for the rest, her shadow of a disdainful smile seemed to stand her in good stead. Clearly as she stood out from among her companions from the first, at the close of the evening she assumed a position actually dramatic.

The big young mountaineer, who, despite his discontent, was a very handsome fellow indeed, had held his own against his rivals stubbornly during the evening, but when, after the final dance, he went in search of his charge, he found that he was not first.

She had fallen into her old attitude against the wall, her hands behind her, and was listening to the appeal of a brawny youth with a hunting-knife in his belt.

"Dusk," he was saying, "I'm not such a chicken hearted chap as to let a gal go back on me. Ye sed I mout hev yer comp'ny home, 'n' I'm a-gwine to hev it, Dave Humes or no Dave Humes."

Dusk merely smiled tolerantly.

"Are ye?" she said.

Rebecca Noble, who stood within a few feet of them, was sure that the lover who approached was the Dave Humes in question, he advanced with such an angry stride, and laying his hand on his rival's shoulder, turned him aside so cavalierly.

"No he aint," he put in; "not an' me about. I brought ye, an' I'll take ye home, Lodusky, or me and him 'll settle it."

The other advanced a step, looking a trifle pale and disheveled. He placed himself square in front of Lodusky.

"Dusk Dunbar," he said, "you're the one to settle it. Which on us is a-gwine home with ye--me or him? Ye haint promised the two of us, hev ye?"

There was certainly a suddenly lit spark of exultation in the girl's coolly dropped eyes.

"Settle it betwixt ye," she answered with her exasperating half smile again.

They had attracted attention by this time, and were becoming the centre figures of a group of lookers-on.

The first had evidently lost his temper. She was the one who should settle it, he proclaimed loudly again. She had promised one man her "comp'ny" and had come with another.

There was so much fierce anger in his face that Miss Noble drew a little nearer, and felt her own blood warmed.

"Which on us is it to be?" he cried.

There was a quick, strong movement on the part of the young man Dave, and he was whirled aside for a second time.

"It's to be me," he was answered. "I'm the man to settle that--I don't leave it to no gal to settle."

In two seconds the lookers-on fell back in dismay, and there was a cry of terror from the women. Two lithe, long-limbed figures were struggling fiercely together, and there was a flash of knives in the air.

Rebecca Noble sprang forward.

"They will kill each other," she said. "Stop them!"

That they would have done each other deadly injury seemed more than probable, but there were cool heads and hands as strong as their own in the room, and in a few minutes they had been dragged apart and stood, each held back by the arms, staring at each other and panting. The lank peacemaker in blue jeans who held Dave Humes shook him gently and with amiable toleration of his folly.

"Look 'ere, boys," he said, "this yere's all a pack of foolishness, ye know--all a pack of foolishness. There aint no sense in it--it's jest foolishness."

Rebecca cast a quick glance at the girl Lodusky. She leaned against the wall just as she had done before; she was as cool as ever, though the spark which hinted at exultation still shone steadily in her eye.

When the two ladies reached the log-cabin at which they had taken up their abode, they found that the story of the event of the evening was before them. Their hostess, whose habit it was to present herself with erratic talk or information at all hours, met them with hospitable eagerness.

"Waal now," she began, "jest to think o' them thar fool boys a-lettin' into one another in thet tharway. I never hearn tell o' sich foolishness. Young folks *is* so foolish. 'N' they drord knives?" This is in the tone of suggestive query.

"Yes," answered Miss Noble, "they drew knives."

"They did!" benignly. "Lord! What fools! Waal now, an' Dusk--what did Dusk do?"

"She stood by and looked on," was the reply.

"Lord!" with the inimitable mountain drawl; "ye don't say so! But it's jest like her--thet is. She's so cur'us, Dusk is. Thar aint no gettin' at her. Ye know the gals ses as she's allers doin' fust one quare thing 'n' then another to get the boys mad at each other. But Lor', p'r'aps 'taint so! Dusk's powerful good-lookin', and gals is jealous, ye know."

"Do you think," questioned Miss Noble, "that they really would have killed each other?"

"Lord! yaas," placidly. "They went to do it. Both Dan'l and Dave's kinder fiery, 'n' they'd nuther on 'em hev give in with Dusk a-lookin' on--they'd hev cut theirselves to pieces fust. Young folks *is* so foolish; gettin' mad about a gal! Lord knows gals is plenty enough."

"Not girls like this one," said Miss Noble, laughing a little.

"Waal now, she *is* good-lookin', aint she? But she's cur'us, Dusk is--she's a cur'us creetur."

"Curious!" echoed Rebecca, finding the term vague even while suggestive.

"Yaas," she said, expansively, "she's cur'us, kinder onsosherble 'n' notionate. Now Dusk is--cur'us. She's so still and sot, 'n' Nath Dunbar and Mandy they think a heap on her,'n' they do the best they kin by her, but she don't never seem to keer about 'em no way. Fur all she's so still, she's powerful sot on fine dressin' an' rich folkses ways. Nath he once tuk her to Asheville, 'n' seems like she's kinder never got over it, but keeps a-broodin' 'bout the way they done thar, 'n' how their clothes looked, 'n' all thet. She knows she's handsum, 'n' she likes to see other folks knows it, though she never says much. I hed to laugh at my Hamp once; Hamp he aint no fool, an' he'd been tuk with her a spell like the rest o' the boys, but he got chock full of her, 'n' one day we was a-talkin,' 'n' the old man he says, 'Waal now, that gal's a hard wad. She's cur'us, 'n' thar's no two ways about it.' An' Hamp he gives a bit of a laugh kinder mad, 'n' he ses, 'Yes, she's cur'us--cur'us as ----!' May be he felt kinder roughed up about her yet--but I hed to laugh."

The next morning Miss Noble devoted to letter-writing. In one of her letters, a bright one, of a tone rather warmer than the rest, she gave her correspondent a very forcible description of the entertainment of the evening before and its closing scene.

"I think it will interest him," she said half aloud, as she wrote upon the envelope the first part of the address, 'Mr. Paul Lennox.'

A shadow falling across the sunshine in the door way checked her and made her look up.

It had rather an arousing effect upon her to find herself confronting the young woman, Lodusky, who stood upon the threshold, regarding her with an air entirely composed, slightly mingled with interest.

"I was in at Mis' Harney's," she remarked, as if the explanation was upon the whole rather superfluous, "'n' I thought I'd come in 'n' see ye."

During her sojourn of three weeks Rebecca had learned enough of the laws of mountain society to understand that the occasion only demanded of her friendliness of demeanor and perfect freedom from ceremony. She rose and placed a chair for her guest.

"I am glad to see you," she said.

Lodusky seated herself.

It was entirely unnecessary to attempt to set her at ease; her composure was perfect. The flaunt-ing-patterned calico must have been a matter of full dress. It had been replaced by a blue-and-white-checked homespun gown--a coarse cotton garment short and scant. Her feet were bare, and their bareness was only a revelation of greater beauty, so perfect was their arched slenderness. Miss Dunbar crossed them with unembarrassed freedom, and looked at the stranger as if she found her worth steady inspection.

"Thet thar's a purty dress you're a-wearin'," she vouchsafed at length.

Rebecca glanced down at her costume. Being a sensible young person, she had attired herself in apparel suitable for mountain rambling. Her dress was simple pilgrim gray, taut made and trim; but she never lost an air of distinction which rendered abundant adornments a secondary matter.

"It is very plain," she answered. "I believe its chief object; is to be as little in the way as possible."

"Taint much trimmed," responded the girl, "but it looks kinder nice, 'n' it sets well. Ye come from the city, Mis' Harney says."

"From New York," said Rebecca. She felt sure that she saw in the tawny brown depths of the girl's eyes a kind of secret eagerness, and this expressed itself openly in her reply.

"I don't blame no one fur wantin' to live in a city," she said, with a kind of discontent. "A body might most as soon be dead as live this way."

Rebecca gave her a keen glance. "Don't you like the quiet?" she asked. "What is it you don't like?"

"I don't like nothin' about it," scornfully. "Thar's nothin' here."

Very slowly a lurking, half-hidden smile showed itself about her fine mouth.

"I'm not goin' to stay here allers," she said.

"You want to go away?" said Rebecca.

She nodded.

"I *am* goin'," she answered, "some o' these days."

"Where?" asked Rebecca, a little coldly, recognizing as she did a repellant element in the girl.

The reply was succinct enough:--

"I don't know whar, 'n' I don't keer whar--but I'm goin'."

She turned her eyes toward the great wall of forest-covered mountain, lifting its height before the open door, and the blood showed its deep glow upon her cheek.

"Some o' these days," she added; "as shore as I'm a woman."

When they talked the matter over afterward, Miss Thorne's remarks were at once decided and severe.

"Shall I tell you what my opinion is, Rebecca?" she said. "It is my opinion that there is evil enough in the creature to be the ruin of the whole community. She is bad at the core."

"I would rather believe," said Rebecca, musingly, "that she was only inordinately vain." Almost instantaneously her musing was broken by a light laugh. "She has dressed her hair as I dress mine," she said, "only it was done better. I could not have arranged it so well. She saw it last night and was quick enough to take in the style at a glance."

At the beginning of the next week there occurred an event which changed materially the ordinary routine of life in the cabin. Heretofore the two sojourners among the mountain fastnesses had walked and climbed under the escort of a small tow-headed Harney. But one evening as she sat sketching on her favorite flat seat of rock, Miss Noble somewhat alarmed this youth by dropping her paper and starting to her feet.

"Orlander" Harney sat and stared at her with black eyes and opened mouth. The red came and went under her fair skin, and she breathed quickly.

"Oh," she cried softly, "how *could* I be mistaken!"

That she was not mistaken became evident immediately. At the very moment she spoke, the advancing horseman, whose appearance had so roused her, glanced upward along the path and caught sight of her figure. He lifted his hat in gay greeting and struck his horse lightly with his whip. Rebecca bent down and picked up her portfolio.

"You may go home," she said quietly to the boy. "I shall be there soon; and you may tell Miss Thorne that Mr. Lennox has come." She was at the base of the rock when the stranger drew rein. "How is this?" she asked with bright uplifted eyes. "We did not think"--

It occurred to Lennox that he had never recognized her peculiar charm so fully as he did at this moment. Rebecca Noble, though not a beauty, possessed a subtle grace of look and air which was not easily resisted,--and just now, as she held out her hand, the clear sweetness of her face shadowed by her piquantly plain hat of rough straw, he felt the influence of this element more strongly than ever before.

"There was no reason why I should not come," he said, "since you did not forbid me."

At sunset they returned to the cabin. Lennox led his rather sorry-looking animal by the bridle, and trusting to its meekness of aspect, devoted his attention wholly to his companion.

"Thet's Nath Dunbar's critter," commented "Mis'" Harney, standing at the door. "They've powerful poor 'commodations fur boardin', but I reckon Nath must 'a' tuk him in."

"Then," said Rebecca, learning that this was the case, "then you have seen Lodusky."

But he had not seen Lodusky, it seemed. She had not been at home when he arrived, and he had only remained in the house long enough to make necessary arrangements before leaving it to go in search of his friends.

The bare, rough-walled room was very cheery that night. Lennox brought with him the gossip of the great world, to which he gave an air of freshness and spice that rendered it very acceptable to the temporary hermits. Outside, the moon shone with a light as clear as day, though softer, and the tender night breezes stirred the pine-tops and nestled among the laurels; inside, by the beautiful barbarous light of the flaring pine-knots on the hearth, two talkers, at least, found the hours fly swiftly.

When these two bade each other good-night it was only natural that they should reach the point toward which they had been veering for twelve months.

Miss Thorne remained in the room, drawing nearer the fire with an amiable little shiver, well excused by the mountain coolness, but Rebecca was beguiled into stepping out into the moonlight The brightness of the moon and the blackness of the shadows cast by trees and rocks and undergrowth, seemed somehow to heighten the effect of the intense and utter stillness reigning around them,--even the occasional distant cry of some wandering wild creature marked, rather than broke in upon, the silence. Rebecca's glance about her was half nervous.

"It is very beautiful," she said, "and it moves one strongly; but I am not sure that it is not, in some of one's moods, just a little oppressive."

It is possible Lennox did not hear her. He was looking down at her with eager eyes. Suddenly he had caught her hand to his lips and kissed it.

"You know why I am here, Rebecca," he said. "Surely, all my hoping is not vain?"

She looked pale and a little startled; but she lifted her face and did not draw herself away.

"Is it?" he asked again. "Have I come on a hopeless errand?"

"No," she answered. "You have not."

His words came freely enough then and with fire. When Rebecca reentered the cabin her large eyes shone in her small, sweet face, and her lips wore a charming curve.

Miss Thorne turned in her chair to look at her and was betrayed into a smile.

"Mr. Lennox has gone, of course," she said.

"Yes."

Then, after a brief silence, in which Rebecca pushed the pine-knots with her foot, the elder lady spoke again.

"Don't you think you may as well tell me about it, Beck, my child?" she said.

Beck looked down and shook her head with very charming gravity.

"Why should I?" she asked. "When--when you know."

Lennox rode his mildly disposed but violently gaited steed homeward in that reposeful state of bliss known only to accepted lovers. He had plucked his flower at last; he was no longer one of the many; he was ecstatically content. Uncertainty had no charm for him, and he was by no means the first discoverer of the subtle fineness her admirers found so difficult to describe in Miss Noble. Granted that she was not a beauty, judged rigidly, still he had found in her soft, clear eye, in her color, her charming voice, even in her little gestures, something which reached him as an artist and touched him as a man.

"One cannot exactly account for other women's paling before her," he said to himself; "but they do--and lose significance." And then he laughed tenderly. At this moment, it was true, every other thing on earth paled and lost significance.

That the family of his host had retired made itself evident to him when he dismounted at the house. To the silence of the night was added the silence of slumber. No one was to be seen; a small cow, rendered lean by active climbing in search of sustenance, breathed peacefully near the tumble-down fence; the ubiquitous, long-legged, yellow dog, rendered trustful by long seclusion, aroused himself from his nap to greet the arrival with a series of heavy raps upon the rickety porch-floor with a solid but languid tail. Lennox stepped over him in reaching for the gourd hanging upon the post, and he did not consider it incumbent upon himself to rise.

In a little hollow at the road-side was the spring from which the household supplies of water were obtained. Finding none in the wooden bucket, Lennox took the gourd with the intention of going down to the hollow to quench his thirst.

"We've powerful good water," his host had said in the afternoon, "'n' it's nigh the house, too. I built the house yer a-purpose,--on 'count of its be-in' nigh."

He was unconsciously dwelling upon this statement as he walked, and trying to recall correctly the mountain drawl and twang.

"She," he said (there was only one "she" for him to-night)--"she will be sure to catch it and reproduce it in all its shades to the life."

He was only a few feet from the spring itself and he stopped with a sharp exclamation of the most uncontrollable amazement,--stopped and stared straight before him. It was a pretty, dell-like place, darkly shadowed on one side but bathed in the flooding moonlight on the other, and it was something he saw in this flood of moonlight which almost caused him to doubt for the moment the evidence of his senses.

How it was possible for him to believe that there really could stand in such a spot a girl attired in black velvet of stagy cut and trimmings, he could not comprehend; but a few feet from him there certainly stood such a girl, who bent her lithe, round shape over the spring, gazing into its depths with all the eagerness of an insatiable vanity.

"I can't see nothing" he heard her say impatiently. "I can't see nothin' nohow."

Despite the beauty, his first glance could not help showing him she was a figure so incongruous and inconsistent as to be almost *bizarre*. When she stood upright revealing fully her tall figure in its shabby finery, he felt something like resentment. He made a restive movement which she heard. The bit of broken looking-glass she held in her hand fell into the water, she uttered a shamefaced angry cry.

"What d'ye want?" she exclaimed. "What are ye a-doin'? I didn't know as no one was a-lookin'. I"--

Her head was flung backward, her full throat looked like a pillar of marble against the black edge of her dress, her air was fierce. He would not have been an artist if he had not been powerfully struck with a sense of her picturesqueness.

But he did not smile at all as he answered:--

"I board at the house there. I returned home late and was thirsty. I came here for water to drink."

Her temper died down as suddenly as it had flamed, and she seemed given up to a miserable, shamed trepidation.

"Oh," she said, "don't ye tell 'em--don't--I--I'm Dusk Dunbar."

Then, as was very natural, he became curious and possibly did smile--a very little.

"What in the name of all that is fantastic are you doing?"

She made an effort at being defiant and succeeded pretty well.

"I wasn't doin' no harm," she said. "I was--dressin' up a bit. It aint nobody's business."

"That's true," he answered coolly. "At all events it is not mine--though it is rather late for a lady to be alone at such a place. However, if you have no objection, I will get what I came for and go back."

She said nothing when he stepped down and filled the gourd, but she regarded him with a sort of irritable watchfulness as he drank.

"Are ye--are ye a-goin' to tell?" she faltered, when he had finished.

"No," he answered as coolly as before. "Why should I?"

Then he gave her a long look from head to foot The dress was a poor enough velveteen and had a cast-off air, but it clung to her figure finely, and its sleeves were picturesque with puffs at the shoulder and slashings of white,--indeed the moonlight made her all black and white; her eyes, which were tawny brown by day, were black as velvet now under the straight lines of her brows, and her face was pure dead fairness itself.

When, his look ended, his eyes met hers, she drew back with an impatient movement. .

"Ye look as if--as if ye thought I didn't get it honest," she exclaimed petulantly, "but I did."

That drew his glance toward her dress again, for of course she referred to that, and he could not help asking her a point-blank question.

"Where *did* you get it?" he said.

There was a slow flippancy about the manner of her reply which annoyed him by its variance with her beauty--but the beauty! How the moonlight and the black and white brought it out as she leaned against the rock, looking at him from under her lashes!

"Are ye goin' to tell the folks up at the house?" she demanded. "They don't know nothin' and I don't want 'em to know."

He shrugged his shoulder negatively.

She laughed with a hint of cool slyness and triumph.

"I got it at Asheville," she said. "I went with father when they was a show thar, 'n' the women stayed at the same tavern we was at, 'n' one of 'em tuk up with me 'n' I done somethin' for her--carried a letter or two," breaking into the sly, triumphant laugh again, "'n' she giv' me the dress fur pay. What d'ye think of it? Is it becomin'?"

The suddenness of the change of manner with which she said these last words was indescribable. She stood upright, her head up, her hands fallen at her sides, her eyes cool and straight--her whole presence confronting him with the power of which she was conscious.

"Is it?" she repeated.

He was a gentleman from instinct and from training, having ordinarily quite a lofty repugnance for all profanity and brusqueness, and yet some how,--account for it as you will,--he had the next instant answered her with positive brutality.

"Yes," he answered, "Damnably!"

When the words were spoken and he heard their sound fall upon the soft night air, he was as keenly disgusted as he would have been if he had heard them uttered by another man. It was not until afterward when he had had leisure to think the matter over that he comprehended vaguely the force which had moved him.

But his companion received them without discomfiture. Indeed, it really occurred to him at the moment that there was a possibility that she would have been less pleased with an expression more choice.

"I come down here to-night," she said, "because I never git no chance to do nothin' up at the house. I'm not a-goin' to let *them* know. Never mind why, but ye mustn't tell 'em."

He felt haughtily anxious to get back to his proper position.

"Why should I?" he said again. "It is no concern of mine."

Then for the first time he noticed the manner in which she had striven to dress her hair in the style of her model, Rebecca Noble, and this irritated him unendurably. He waved his hand toward it with a gesture of distaste.

"Don't do that again," he said. "That is not becoming at least "--though he was angrily conscious that it was.

She bent over the spring with a hint of alarm in her expression.

"Aint it?" she said, and the eager rapidity with which she lifted her hands and began to alter it almost drew a smile from him despite his mood.

"I done it like hern," she began, and stopped suddenly to look up at him. "You know her," she added; "they're at Harney's. Father said ye'd went to see her jest as soon as ye got here."

"I know her," was his short reply.

He picked up the drinking-gourd and turned away.

"Good-night," he said.

"Good-night."

At the top of the rocky incline he looked back at her.

She was kneeling upon the brink of the spring, her sleeve pushed up to her shoulder, her hand and arm in the water, dipping for the fragment of looking-glass.

It was really not wholly inconsistent that he should not directly describe the interview in his next meeting with his betrothed. Indeed, Rebecca was rather struck by the coolness with which he treated the subject when he explained that he had seen the girl and found her beauty all it had been painted.

"Is it possible," she asked, "that she did not quite please you?"

"Are you sure," he returned, "that she quite pleases *you?*"

Rebecca gave a moment to reflection.

"But her beauty"--she began, when it was over.

"Oh!" he interposed, "as a matter of color and curve and proportion she is perfect; one must admit that, however reluctantly."

Rebecca laughed.

"Why 'reluctantly?'" she said.

It was his turn to give a moment to reflection.

His face shadowed, and he looked a little disturbed.

"I don't know," he replied at length; "I give it up."

He had expected to see a great deal of the girl, but somehow he saw her even oftener than he had anticipated. During the time he spent in the house, chance seemed to throw her continually in his path or under his eye. From his window he saw her carrying water from the spring, driving the small agile cow to and from the mountain pasturage, or idling in the shade. Upon the whole it was oftener this last than any other occupation. With her neglected knitting in her hands she would sit for hours under a certain low-spreading cedar not far from the door, barefooted, coarsely clad, beautiful,--every tinge of the sun, every indifferent leisurely movement, a new suggestion of a new grace.

It would have been impossible to resist the temptation to watch her; and this Lennox did at first almost unconsciously. Then he did more. One beautiful still morning she stood under the cedar, her hand thrown lightly above her head to catch at a bough, and as she remained motionless, he made a sketch of her. When it was finished he was seized with the whimsical impulse to go out and show it to her.

She took it with an uncomprehending air, but the moment she saw what it was a flush of triumph and joy lighted up her face.

"It's me," she cried in a low, eager voice. "Me! Do I look like that thar? Do I?"

"You look as that would look if it had color, and was more complete."

She glanced up at him sharply.

"D'ye mean if it was han'somer?"

He was tempted into adding to her excitement with a compliment.

"Yes," he said, "very much handsomer than I could ever hope to make it."

A slow, deep red rose to her face.

"Give it to me!" she demanded.

"If you will stand in the same position until I have drawn another--certainly," he returned.

He was fully convinced that when she repeated the attitude there would be added to it a look of consciousness.

When she settled into position and caught at the bough again, he watched in some distaste for the growth of the nervously complaisant air, but it did not appear. She was unconsciousness itself.

It is possible that Rebecca Noble had never been so happy during her whole life as she was during this one summer. Her enjoyment of every wild beauty and novelty was immeasurably keen. Just at this time to be shut out, and to be as it were high above the world, added zest to her pleasure.

"Ah," she said once to her lover, "happiness is better here--one can taste it slowly."

Fatigue seemed impossible to her. With Lennox as her companion she performed miracles in the way of walking and climbing, and explored the mountain fastnesses for miles around. Her step grew firm and elastic, her color richer, her laugh had a buoyant ring. She had never been so nearly a beautiful woman as she was sometimes when she came back to the cabin after a ramble, bright and sun-flushed, her hands full of laurel and vines.

"Your gown of 'hodden-gray' is wonderfully becoming, Beck," Lennox said again and again with a secret exulting pride in her.

Their plans for the future took tone from their blissful, unconventional life. They could not settle down until they had seen the world. They would go here and there, and perhaps, if they found it pleasanter so, not settle down at all. There were certain clay-white, closely built villages, whose tumble-down houses jostled each other upon divers precipitous cliffs on the wayside between Florence and Rome, toward which Lennox's compass seemed always to point. He rather argued that the fact of their not being dilated upon in the guide-books rendered them additionally interesting. Rebecca had her fancies too, and together they managed to talk a good deal of tender, romantic nonsense, which was purely their own business, and gave the summer days a delicate yet distinct flavor.

The evening after the sketch was made they spent upon the mountain side together. When they stopped to rest, Lennox flung himself upon the ground at Rebecca's feet, and lay looking up at the far away blue of the sky in which a slow-flying bird circled lazily. Rebecca, with a cluster of pink and white laurel in her hand, proceeded with a metaphysical and poetical harangue she had previously begun.

"To my eyes," she said, "it has a pathetic air of loneliness--pathetic and yet not exactly sorrowful. It knows nothing but its own pure, brave, silent life. It is only pathetic to a worldling--worldlings like us. How fallen we must be to find a life desolate because it has only nature for a companion!"

She stopped with an idle laugh, waiting for an ironical reply from the "worldling" at her feet; but he remained silent, still looking upward at the clear, deep blue.

As she glanced toward him she saw something lying upon the grass between them, and bent to pick it up. It was the sketch which he had forgotten and which had slipped from the portfolio.

"You have dropped something," she said, and seeing what it was, uttered an exclamation of pleasure.

He came back to earth with a start, and, recognizing the sketch, looked more than half irritated.

"Oh, it is that, is it?" he said.

"It is perfect!" she exclaimed. "What a pictare it will make!"

"It is not to be a picture," he answered. "It was not intended to be anything more than a sketch."

"But why not?" she asked. "It is too good to lose. You never had such a model in your life before."

"No," he answered grudgingly.

The hand with which Rebecca held the sketch dropped. She turned her attention to her lover, and a speculative interest grew in her face.

"That girl"--she said slowly, after a mental summing up occupying a few seconds--"that girl irritates you--irritates you."

He laughed faintly.

"I believe she does," he replied; "yes, 'irritates' is the word to use."

And yet if this were true, his first act upon returning home was a singular one.

He was rather late, but the girl Lodusky was sitting in the moonlight at the door. He stopped and spoke to her.

"If I should wish to paint you," he said rather coldly, "would you do me the favor of sitting to me?"

She did not answer him at once, but seemed to weigh his words as she looked out across the moonlight.

"Ye mean, will I let ye put me in a picter?" she said at last.

He nodded.

"Yes," she answered.

"I reckon he told ye he was a-paintin' Dusk's picter," "Mis'" Harney said to her boarders a week later.

"Mr. Lennox?" returned Rebecca; "yes, he told us."

"I thort so," nodding benignly. "Waal now, Dusk'll make a powerful nice picter if she don't git contrairy. The trouble with Dusk is her a-gittin' contrairy. She's as like old Hance Dunbar as she kin be. I mean in some ways. Lord knows, 'twouldn't do to say she was like him in everythin'."

Naturally, Miss Noble made some inquiries into the nature of old Hance Dunbar's "contrairiness." Secretly, she had a desire to account for Lodusky according to established theory.

"I wonder ye haint heern of him," said Mis Harney. "He was just awful--old Hance! He was Nath's daddy, an' Lord! the wickedest feller! Folks was afeared of him. No one darsn't to go a-nigh him when he'd git mad--a-rippin' 'n' a-rearin' 'n' a-chargin'.. 'N' he never got no religion, mind ye; he died jest that a-way. He was allers a hankerin' arter seein' the world, 'n' he went off an' stayed off a right smart while,--nine or ten year,--'n' lived in all sorts o' ways in them big cities. When he come back he was a sight to see, sick 'n' pore 'n' holler-eyed, but as wicked as ever. Dusk was a little thing 'n' he was a old man, but he'd laugh 'n' tell her to take care of her face 'n' be a smart gal. He was drefful sick at last 'n' suffered a heap, 'n' one day he got up offen his bed 'n' tuk down Nath's gun 'n' shot hisself as cool as could be. He hadn't no patience, 'n' he said, 'When a G--derned man had lived through what he had 'n' then wouldn't die, it was time to kill him.' Seems like it sorter 'counts fur Dusk; she don't git her cur'usness from her own folks; Nath an' Mandy's mighty clever, both on 'em."

"Perhaps it does 'count for Dusk," Rebecca said, after telling the tale to Lennox. "It must be a fearful thing to have such blood in one's veins and feel it on fire. Let us," she continued with a smile, "be as charitable as possible."

When the picture was fairly under way, Lennox's visits to the Harneys' cabin were somewhat less frequent. The mood in which she found he had gradually begun to regard his work aroused in Rebecca a faint wonder. He seemed hardly to like it, and yet to be fascinated by it. He was averse to speaking freely of it, and still he thought of it continually. Frequently when they were together, he wore an absent, perturbed air.

"You do not look content," she said to him once.

He passed his hand quickly across his forehead and smiled, plainly with an effort, but he made no reply.

The picture progressed rather slowly upon the whole. Rebecca had thought the subject a little fantastic at first, and yet had been attracted by it. A girl in a peculiar dress of black and white bent over a spring with an impatient air, trying in vain to catch a glimpse of her beauty in the reflection of the moonlight.

"It 's our spring, shore," commented "Mis'" Dunbar. "'N' its Dusk--but Lord! how fine she's fixed. Ye're as fine as ye want to be in the picter, Dusk, if ye wa'n't never fine afore. Don't ye wish ye had sich dressin' as thet thar now?"

The sittings were at the outset peculiarly silent. There was no untimely motion or change of expression, and yet no trying passiveness. The girl gave any position a look of unconsciousness quite wonderful. Privately, Lennox was convinced that she was an actress from habit--that her ease was the result of life-long practice. Sometimes he found his own consciousness of her steady gaze almost unbearable. He always turned to meet her deep eyes fixed upon him with an expression he could not fathom. Frequently he thought it an expression of dislike--of secret resentment--of subtle defiance. There came at last a time when he knew that he turned toward her again and again because he felt that he must--because he had a feverish wish to see if the look had changed.

Once when he did this he saw that it *had* changed. She had moved a little, her eyes were dilated with a fire which startled him beyond self-control, her color came and went, she breathed fast. The next instant she sprang from her chair.

"I wont stand it no longer," she cried panting: "no longer--I wont!"

Her ire was magnificent. She flung her head back, and struck her side with her clinched hand.

"No longer!" she said; "not a minute!"

Lennox advanced one step and stood, palette in hand, gazing at her.

"What have I done?" he asked. "What?"

"What?" she echoed with contemptuous scorn. "Nothin'! ***But d'ye think I don't know ye?***"

"Know me!" he repeated after her mechanically, finding it impossible to remove his glance from her.

"What d'ye take me me fur?" she demanded. "A fool? Yes, I was a fool--a fool to come here, 'n' set 'n' let ye--let ye despise me!" in a final outburst.

Still he could only echo her again, and say "Despise you!"

Her voice lowered itself into an actual fierceness of tone.

"Ye've done it from first to last," she said. "Would ye look at her like ye look at me? Would ye turn half way 'n' look at her, 'n' then turn back as if--as if--. Aint there"--her eyes ablaze--"aint there no *life*--to me?"

"Stop!" he began hoarsely.

"I'm beneath her, am I?" she persisted. "Me beneath another woman--Dusk Dunbar! It's the first time!"

She walked toward the door as if to leave him, but suddenly she stopped. A passionate tremor shook her; he saw her throat swell. She threw her arm up against the logs of the wall and dropped her face upon it sobbing tumultuously.

There was a pause of perhaps three seconds. Then Lennox moved slowly toward her. Almost unconsciously he laid his hand upon her heaving shoulder and so stood trembling a little.

When Rebecca paid her next visit to the picture it struck her that it appeared at a standstill. As she looked at it her lover saw a vague trouble growing slowly in her eyes.

"What!" he remarked. "It does not please you?"

"I think," she answered,--"I feel as if it had not pleased you."

He fell back a few paces and stood scanning it with an impression at once hard and curious.

"Please me!" he exclaimed in a voice almost strident. "It should. She has beauty enough."

On her return home that day Rebecca drew forth from the recesses of her trunk her neglected writing folio and a store of paper.

Miss Thorne, entering the room, found her kneeling over her trunk, and spoke to her.

"What are you going to do?" she asked.

Rebecca smiled faintly.

"What I ought to have begun before," she said. "I am behindhand with my work."

She laid the folio and her inkstand upon the table, and made certain methodical arrangements for her labor. She worked diligently all day, and looked slightly pale and wearied when she rose from her seat in the evening. Until eleven o'clock she sat at the open door, sometimes talking quietly, sometimes silent and listening to the wind among the pines. She did, not mention her lover's name, and he did not come. She spent many a day and night in the same manner after this. For the present the long, idle rambles and unconventional moon-lit talks were over. It was tacitly understood between herself and her aunt that Lennox's labor occupied him.

"It seems a strange time to begin a picture--during a summer holiday," said Miss Thorne a little sharply upon one occasion.

Rebecca laughed with an air of cheer.

"No time is a strange time to an artist," she answered. "Art is a mistress who gives no holidays."

She was continually her bright, erect, alert self. The woman who loved her dearly and had known her from her earliest childhood, found her sagacity and knowledge set at naught as it were. She had been accustomed to see her niece admired far beyond the usual lot of women; she had gradually learned to feel it only natural that she should inspire quite a strong sentiment even in casual acquaintances. She had felt the delicate power of her fascination herself, but never at her best and brightest had she found her more charming or quicker of wit and fancy than she was now.

Even Lennox, coming every few days with a worn-out look and touched with a haggard shadow, made no outward change in her.

"She does not look," said the elder lady to herself, "like a neglected woman." And then the sound of the phrase struck her with a sharp incredulous pain. "A neglected woman!" she repeated,--"Beck!"

She did not understand, and was not weak enough to ask questions.

Lennox came and went, and Rebecca gained upon her work until she could no longer say she was behindhand. The readers of her letters and sketches found them fresh and sparkling, "as if," wrote a friend, "you were braced both mentally and physically by the mountain air."

But once in the middle of the night Miss Thorne awakened with a mysterious shock to find the place at her side empty, and her niece sitting at the open window in a quiet which suggested that she might not have moved for an hour.

She obeyed her strong first impulse, and rose and went to her.

She laid her hand on her shoulder, and shook her gently.

"Beck!" she demanded, "what are you doing?"

When the girl turned slowly round, she started sit the sight of her cold, miserable pallor.

"I am doing nothing--nothing," she answered. "Why did you get up? It's a fine night, isn't it?"

Despite her discretion, Miss Thorne broke down into a blunder.

"You--you never look like this in the daytime!" she exclaimed.

"No," was the reply given with cool deliberateness. "No; I would rather *die*."

For the moment she was fairly incomprehensible. There was in the set of her eye and the expression of her fair, clear face, the least hint of dogged obstinacy.

"Beck "--she began.

"You ought not to have got up," said Beck. "It is enough to look 'like this' at night when I am by myself. Go back to bed, if you please."

Miss Thorne went back to bed meekly. She was at once alarmed and subdued. She felt as if she had had a puzzling interview with a stranger.

In these days Lennox regarded his model with morbid interest. A subtle change was perceptible in her. Her rich color deepened, she held herself more erect, her eye had a larger pride and light. She was a finer creature than ever, and yet--she came at his call. He never ceased to wonder at it. Sometimes the knowledge of his power stirred within him a vast impatience; sometimes he was hardened by it; but somehow it never touched him, though he was thrown into tumult--bound against his will. He could not say that he understood her. Her very passiveness baffled him and caused him to ask himself what it meant. She spoke little, and her emotional phases seemed reluctant, but her motionless face and slowly raised eye always held a meaning of their own.

On an occasion when he mentioned his approaching departure, she started as if she had received a blow, and he turned to see her redden and pale alternately, her face full of alarm.

"What is the matter?" he asked brusquely.

"I--hadn't bin thinkin' on it," she stammered. "I'd kinder forgot."

He turned to his easel again and painted rapidly for a few minutes. Then he felt a light touch on his arm. She had left her seat noiselessly and stood beside him. She gave him a passionate, protesting look. A fire of excitement seemed to have sprung up within her and given her a defiant daring.

"D'ye think I'll stay here--when ye're gone--like I did before?" she said.

She had revealed herself in many curious lights to him, but no previous revelation had been so wonderful as was the swift change of mood and bearing which took place in her at this instant. In a moment she had melted into soft tears, her lips were tremulous, her voice dropped into a shaken whisper.

"I've allers wanted to go away," she said. "I--I've allers said I would. I want to go to a city somewhar--I don't keer whar. I might git work--I've heerd of folks as did. P'r'aps some un ud hire me!"

He stared at her like a man fascinated.

"You go to the city alone!" he said under his breath. "You try to get work!"

"Yes," she answered. "Don't ye know no one"--

He stopped her.

"No," he said, "I don't. It would be a dangerous business unless you had friends. As for me, I shall not be in America long. As soon as I am married I go with my wife to Europe."

He heard a sharp click in her throat. Her tears were dried, and she was looking straight at him.

"Are ye a-goin' to be married?" she asked.

"Yes."

"To--her?" with a gesture in the direction of the Harneys' cabin.

"Yes."

"Oh!" and she walked out of the room.

He did not see her for three days, and the picture stood still. He went to the Harneys' and found Rebecca packing her trunk.

"We are going back to New York," she said.

"Why?" he asked.

"Because our holiday is over."

Miss Thorne regarded him with chill severity.

"When may we expect to see you?" she inquired.

He really felt half stupefied,--as if for the time being his will was paralyzed.

"I don't know," he answered.

He tried to think that he was treated badly and coldly. He told himself that he had done nothing to deserve this style of thing, that he had simply been busy and absorbed in his work, and that if he had at times appeared preoccupied it was not to be wondered at. But when he looked at Rebecca he did not put these thoughts into words; he did not even say that of course he should follow them soon, since there was nothing to detain him but a sketch or two he had meant to make.

By night they were gone and he was left restless and miserable. He was so restless that he could not sleep but wandered down toward the spring. He stopped at the exact point at which he had stopped on the night of his arrival--at the top of the zigzag little path leading down the rocky incline. He stopped because he heard a sound of passionate sobbing. He descended slowly. He knew the sound--angry, fierce, uncontrollable--because he had heard it before. It checked itself the instant he reached the ground. Lodusky leaning against a projecting rock kept her eyes fixed upon the water.

"Why did you come here?" he demanded, a little excitedly. "What are you crying for? What has hurt you?"

"Nothing" in a voice low and unsteady.

He drew a little nearer to her and for the first time was touched. She would not look at him, she was softened and altered, in her whole appearance, by a new pallor.

"Have "--he began, "have I?"

"You!" she cried, turning on him with a bitter, almost wild gesture. "You wouldn't keer if I was struck *dead* afore ye!"

"Look here," he said to her, with an agitation he could not master. "Let me tell you something about myself. If you think I am a passably good fellow you are mistaken. I am a bad fellow, a poor fellow, an ignoble fellow. You don't understand?" as she gazed at him in bewilderment. "No, of course, you don't. God knows I didn't myself until within the last two weeks. It's folly to say such things to you; perhaps I say them half to satisfy myself. But I mean to show you that I am not to be trusted. I think perhaps I am too poor a fellow to love any woman honestly and altogether. I followed one woman here, and then after all let another make me waver"--

"Another!" she faltered.

He fixed his eyes on her almost coldly.

"You," he said.

He seemed to cast the word at her and wonder what she would make of it He waited a second or so before he went on.

"You, and yet you are not the woman I love either. Good God! What a villain I must be. I am an insult to every woman that breathes. It is not even you--though I can't break from you, and you have made me despise myself. There! do you know now--do you see now that I am not worth "--

The next instant he started backward. Before he had time for a thought she had uttered a low cry, and flung herself down at his feet.

"I don't keer," she panted; "I wont keer fur nothin',--whether ye're good or bad,--only don't leave me here when ye go away."

*****

A week later Lennox arose one morning and set about the task of getting his belongings together. He had been up late and had slept heavily and long. He felt exhausted and looked so.

The day before, his model had given him his last sitting. The picture stood finished upon the easel. It was a thorough and artistic piece of work, and yet the sight of it was at times unbearable to him. There were times again, however, when it fascinated him anew when he went and stood opposite to it, regarding it with an intense gaze. He scarcely knew how the last week had passed. It seemed to have been spent in alternate feverish struggles and reckless abandonment to impulse. He had let himself drift here and there, he had at last gone so far as to tell himself that the time had arrived when baseness was possible to him.

"I don't promise you an easy life," he had said to Dusk the night before. "I tell you I am a bad fellow, and I have lost something through you that I cared for. You may wish yourself back again."

"If you leave me," she said, "I'll kill myself!" and she struck her hands together.

For the moment he was filled, as he often was, with a sense of passionate admiration. It was true he saw her as no other creature had ever seen her before, that so far as such a thing was possible with her, she loved him--loved him with a fierce, unreserved, yet narrow passion.

He had little actual packing to do--merely the collecting of a few masculine odds and ends, and then his artistic accompaniments. Nothing was of consequence but these; the rest were tossed together indifferently, but the picture was to be left until the last moment, that its paint might be dry beyond a doubt.

Having completed his preparations he went out. He had the day before him, and scarcely knew what to do with it, but it must be killed in one way or another. He wandered up the mountain and at last lay down with his cigar among the laurels. He was full of a strange excitement which now thrilled, now annoyed him.

He came back in the middle of the afternoon and laughed a rather half-hearted laugh at the excellent Mandy's comment upon his jaded appearance.

"Ye look kinder tuckered out," she said. "Ye'd oughtn't ter walked so fur when ye was a-gwine off to-night. Ye'd orter rested."

She stopped the churn-dasher and regarded him with a good-natured air of interest.

"Hev ye seed Dusk to say good-by to her?" she added. "She's went over the mountain ter help Mirandy Stillins with her soap. She wont be back fur a day or two."

He went into his room and shut the door. A fierce repulsion sickened him. He had heretofore held himself with a certain degree of inward loftiness; he had so condemned the follies and sins of other men, and here he found himself involved in a low and common villainy, in the deceits which belonged to his crime, and which preyed upon simplicity and ignorant trust.

He went and stood before his easel, hot with a blush of self-scorn.

"Has it come to this?" he muttered through his clinched teeth--"to ***this!***"

He made an excited forward movement; his foot touched the supports of the easel, jarring it roughly; the picture fell upon the floor.

"What?" he cried out. "Beck! You! Great God!"

For before him, revealed by the picture's fall, the easel held one of the fairest memories he had of the woman he had proved himself too fickle and slight to value rightly. It was merely a sketch made rapidly one day soon after his arrival and never wholly completed, but it had been touched with fire and feeling, and the face looked out from the canvas with eyes whose soft happiness stung him to the quick with the memories they brought. He had meant to finish it, and had left it upon the easel that he might turn to it at any moment, and it had remained there, covered by a stronger rival--forgotten.

He sat down in a chair and his brow fell upon his hands. He felt as if he had been clutched and dragged backward by a powerful arm.

When at last he rose, he strode to the picture lying upon the floor, ground it under his heel, and spurned it from him with an imprecation.

He was, at a certain hour, to reach a particular bend in the road some miles distant. He was to walk to this place and if he found no one there, to wait.

When at sunset that evening he reached it, he was half an hour before the time specified, but he was not the first at the tryst. He was within twenty yards of the spot when a figure rose from the roots of a tree and stood waiting for him--the girl Dusk with a little bundle in her hand.

She was not flushed or tremulous with any hint of mental excitement; she awaited him with a fine repose, even the glow of the dying sun having no power to add to her color, but as he drew near he saw her look gradually change. She did not so much as stir, but the change grew slowly, slowly upon her face, and developed there into definite shape--the shape of secret, repressed dread.

"What is it," she asked when he at last confronted her, "that ails ye?"

She uttered the words in a half whisper, as if she had not the power to speak louder, and he saw the hand hanging at her side close itself.

"What is it--that ails ye?"

He waited a few seconds before he answered her.

"Look at me," he said at last, "and see."

She did look at him. For the space of ten seconds their eyes were fixed upon each other in a long, bitter look. Then her little bundle dropped on the ground.

"Ye've went back on me," she said under her breath again. "Ye've went back on me!"

He had thought she might make some passionate outcry, but she did not yet. A white wrath was in her face and her chest heaved, but she spoke slowly and low, her hands fallen down by her side.

"Ye've went back on me," she said. "An' *I knew ye would*."

He felt that the odor of his utter falseness tainted the pure air about him; he had been false all round,--to himself, to his love, to his ideals,--even in a baser way here.

"Yes," he answered her with a bitterness she did not understand, "I've gone back on you." Then, as if to himself, "I could not even reach perfection in villainy."

Then her rage and misery broke forth.

"Yer a coward!" she said, with gasps between her words. "Yer afraid! I'd sooner--I'd sooner ye'd killed me--dead!"

Her voice shrilled itself into a smothered shriek, she cast herself face downward upon the earth and lay there clutching amid her sobs at the grass.

He looked down at her in a cold, stunned fashion.

"Do you think," he said hoarsely, "that you can loathe me as I loathe myself? Do you think you can call me one shameful name I don't know I deserve? If you can, for God's sake let me have it."

She struck her fist against the earth.

"Thar wasn't a man I ever saw," she said, "that didn't foller after me, 'n' do fur me, 'n' wait fur a word from me. They'd hev let me set my foot on 'em if I'd said it. Thar wasn't nothin' I mightn't hev done--not nothin'. An' now--an' now "--and, she tore the grass from its earth and flung it from her.

"Go on," he said. "Go on and say your worst."

Her worst was bad enough, but he almost exulted under the blows she dealt him. He felt the horrible sting a vague comfort. He had fallen low enough surely when it was a comfort to be told that he was a liar, a poltroon, and a scoundrel.

The sun had been down an hour when it was over and she had risen and taken up her bundle.

"Why don't ye ask me to forgive ye?" she said with a scathing sneer. "Why don't ye ask me to forgive ye--an' say ye didn't mean to do it?"

He fell back a pace and was silent. With what grace would the words have fallen from his lips? And yet he knew that he had not **meant** to do it.

She turned away and at a distance of a few feet stopped. She gave him a last look--a fierce one in its contempt and anger, and her affluence of beauty had never been so stubborn a fact before.

"Ye think ye've left me behind," she said. "An' so ye hev--but it aint fur allers. The time'll come when mebbe ye'll see me ag'in."

He returned to New York, but he had been there a week before he went to Rebecca. Finally, however, he awoke one morning feeling that the time had come for the last scene of his miserable drama. He presented himself at the house and sent up his name, and in three minutes Rebecca came to him.

It struck him with a new thrill of wretchedness to see that she wore by chance the very dress she had worn the day he had made the sketch--a pale, pure-looking gray, with a scarf of white lace loosely fastened at her throat. Next, he saw that there was a painful change in her, that she looked frail and worn, as if she had been ill. His first words he scarcely heard and never remembered. He had not come to make a defense, but a naked, bitter confession. As he made it low and monotonously, in brief, harsh words, holding no sparing for himself, Rebecca stood with her hand upon the mantle looking at him with simple directness. There was no rebuke in her look, but there was weariness. It occurred to him once or twice and with a terribly humiliating pang, that she was tired of him,--tired of it all.

"I have lost you," he ended. "And I have lost myself. I have seen myself as I am,--a poorer figure, a grosser one than I ever dreamed of being, even in the eyes of my worst enemy. Henceforth, this figure will be my companion. It is as if I looked at myself in a bad glass; but now, though the reflection is a pitiable one, the glass is true."

"You think," she said, after a short silence, "of going away?"

"Yes."

"Where?"

"To Europe."

"Oh," she ejaculated, with a soft, desperate sound of pain.

His eyes had been downcast and he raised them.

"Yes," he said, mournfully. "We were to have gone together."

"Yes," she answered, "together."

Her eyes were wet.

"I was very happy," she said, "for a little while."

She held out her hand.

"But," she added, as if finishing a sentence, "you have been truer to me than you think."

"No--no," he groaned.

"Yes, truer to me than you think--and truer to yourself. It was I you loved--I! There have been times when I thought I must give that up, but now I know I need not. It was I. Sometime, perhaps,--sometime,--not now"--

Her voice broke, she did not finish, the end was a sob. Their eyes rested upon each other a few seconds, and then he released her hand and went away.

He was absent for two years, and during that time his friends heard much good of him. He lived the life of a recluse and a hard worker. He learned to know his own strength, and taught the world to recognize it also.

At the end of the second year, being in Paris, he went one night to the ***Nouvelle Opera***. Toward the close of the second act he became conscious of a little excited stir among those surrounding him. Every glass seemed directed toward a new arrival who stood erect and cool in one of the stage-boxes. She might have been Cleopatra. Her costume was of a creamy satin, she was covered with jewels, and she stood up confronting the house, as it regarded her, with ***sang froid***.

Lennox rose hurriedly and left the place. He was glad to breathe the bitterly cold but pure night air. She had made no idle prophecy. He had seen her again!

There hung upon the wall of his private room a picture whose completion had been the first work after his landing. He went in to it and looked at it with something like adoration.

"'Sometime'" he said, "perhaps now," and the next week he was on his way home.

The Codes Of Hammurabi And Moses
W. W. Davies

QTY

The discovery of the Hammurabi Code is one of the greatest achievements of archaeology, and is of paramount interest, not only to the student of the Bible, but also to all those interested in ancient history...

Religion   **ISBN:** *1-59462-338-4*   **Pages:132**
MSRP $12.95

The Theory of Moral Sentiments
Adam Smith

QTY

This work from 1749. contains original theories of conscience amd moral judgment and it is the foundation for systemof morals.

Philosophy **ISBN:** *1-59462-777-0*   **Pages:536**
MSRP $19.95

Jessica's First Prayer
Hesba Stretton

QTY

In a screened and secluded corner of one of the many railway-bridges which span the streets of London there could be seen a few years ago, from five o'clock every morning until half past eight, a tidily set-out coffee-stall, consisting of a trestle and board, upon which stood two large tin cans, with a small fire of charcoal burning under each so as to keep the coffee boiling during the early hours of the morning when the work-people were thronging into the city on their way to their daily toil...

Childrens **ISBN:** *1-59462-373-2*   **Pages:84**
MSRP $9.95

My Life and Work
Henry Ford

QTY

Henry Ford revolutionized the world with his implementation of mass production for the Model T automobile. Gain valuable business insight into his life and work with his own auto-biography... "We have only started on our development of our country we have not as yet, with all our talk of wonderful progress, done more than scratch the surface. The progress has been wonderful enough but..."

Biographies/ **ISBN:** *1-59462-198-5*   **Pages:300**
MSRP $21.95

The Art of Cross-Examination
Francis Wellman

QTY

I presume it is the experience of every author, after his first book is published upon an important subject, to be almost overwhelmed with a wealth of ideas and illustrations which could readily have been included in his book, and which to his own mind, at least, seem to make a second edition inevitable. Such certainly was the case with me; and when the first edition had reached its sixth impression in five months, I rejoiced to learn that it seemed to my publishers that the book had met with a sufficiently favorable reception to justify a second and considerably enlarged edition. ..

Pages:412

Reference   **ISBN: *1-59462-647-2***   *MSRP $19.95*

On the Duty of Civil Disobedience
Henry David Thoreau

QTY

Thoreau wrote his famous essay, On the Duty of Civil Disobedience, as a protest against an unjust but popular war and the immoral but popular institution of slave-owning. He did more than write—he declined to pay his taxes, and was hauled off to gaol in consequence. Who can say how much this refusal of his hastened the end of the war and of slavery ?

Law   **ISBN: *1-59462-747-9***   **Pages:48**

MSRP $7.45

Dream Psychology Psychoanalysis for Beginners
Sigmund Freud

QTY

Sigmund Freud, born Sigismund Schlomo Freud (May 6, 1856 - September 23, 1939), was a Jewish-Austrian neurologist and psychiatrist who co-founded the psychoanalytic school of psychology. Freud is best known for his theories of the unconscious mind, especially involving the mechanism of repression; his redefinition of sexual desire as mobile and directed towards a wide variety of objects; and his therapeutic techniques, especially his understanding of transference in the therapeutic relationship and the presumed value of dreams as sources of insight into unconscious desires.

Pages:196

Psychology   **ISBN: *1-59462-905-6***   *MSRP $15.45*

The Miracle of Right Thought
Orison Swett Marden

QTY

Believe with all of your heart that you will do what you were made to do. When the mind has once formed the habit of holding cheerful, happy, prosperous pictures, it will not be easy to form the opposite habit. It does not matter how improbable or how far away this realization may see, or how dark the prospects may be, if we visualize them as best we can, as vividly as possible, hold tenaciously to them and vigorously struggle to attain them, they will gradually become actualized, realized in the life. But a desire, a longing without endeavor, a yearning abandoned or held indifferently will vanish without realization.

Pages:360

Self Help   **ISBN: *1-59462-644-8***   *MSRP $25.45*

The Rosicrucian Cosmo-Conception Mystic Christianity *by Max Heindel*   ISBN: *1-59462-188-8*   **$38.95**
The Rosicrucian Cosmo-conception is not dogmatic, neither does it appeal to any other authority than the reason of the student. It is: not controversial, but is: sent forth in the, hope that it may help to clear...   New Age/Religion Pages 646

Abandonment To Divine Providence *by Jean-Pierre de Caussade*   ISBN: *1-59462-228-0*   **$25.95**
"The Rev. Jean Pierre de Caussade was one of the most remarkable spiritual writers of the Society of Jesus in France in the 18th Century. His death took place at Toulouse in 1751. His works have gone through many editions and have been republished...   Inspirational/Religion Pages 400

Mental Chemistry *by Charles Haanel*   ISBN: *1-59462-192-6*   **$23.95**
Mental Chemistry allows the change of material conditions by combining and appropriately utilizing the power of the mind. Much like applied chemistry creates something new and unique out of careful combinations of chemicals the mastery of mental chemistry...   New Age Pages 354

The Letters of Robert Browning and Elizabeth Barret Barrett 1845-1846 vol II   ISBN: *1-59462-193-4*   **$35.95**
by Robert Browning and Elizabeth Barrett   Biographies Pages 596

Gleanings In Genesis (volume I) *by Arthur W. Pink*   ISBN: *1-59462-130-6*   **$27.45**
Appropriately has Genesis been termed "the seed plot of the Bible" for in it we have, in germ form, almost all of the great doctrines which are afterwards fully developed in the books of Scripture which follow...   Religion/Inspirational Pages 420

The Master Key *by L. W. de Laurence*   ISBN: *1-59462-001-6*   **$30.95**
In no branch of human knowledge has there been a more lively increase of the spirit of research during the past few years than in the study of Psychology, Concentration and Mental Discipline. The requests for authentic lessons in Thought Control, Mental Discipline and...   New Age/Business Pages 422

The Lesser Key Of Solomon Goetia *by L. W. de Laurence*   ISBN: *1-59462-092-X*   **$9.95**
This translation of the first book of the "Lernegton" which is now for the first time made accessible to students of Talismanic Magic was done, after careful collation and edition, from numerous Ancient Manuscripts in Hebrew, Latin, and French...   New Age/Occult Pages 92

Rubaiyat Of Omar Khayyam *by Edward Fitzgerald*   ISBN:*1-59462-332-5*   **$13.95**
Edward Fitzgerald, whom the world has already learned, in spite of his own efforts to remain within the shadow of anonymity, to look upon as one of the rarest poets of the century, was born at Bredfield, in Suffolk, on the 31st of March, 1809. He was the third son of John Purcell...   Music Pages 172

Ancient Law *by Henry Maine*   ISBN: *1-59462-128-4*   **$29.95**
The chief object of the following pages is to indicate some of the earliest ideas of mankind, as they are reflected in Ancient Law, and to point out the relation of those ideas to modern thought.   Religiom/History Pages 452

Far-Away Stories *by William J. Locke*   ISBN: *1-59462-129-2*   **$19.45**
"Good wine needs no bush, but a collection of mixed vintages does. And this book is just such a collection. Some of the stories I do not want to remain buried for ever in the museum files of dead magazine-numbers an author's not unpardonable vanity..."   Fiction Pages 272

Life of David Crockett *by David Crockett*   ISBN: *1-59462-250-7*   **$27.45**
"Colonel David Crockett was one of the most remarkable men of the times in which he lived. Born in humble life, but gifted with a strong will, an indomitable courage, and unremitting perseverance...   Biographies/New Age Pages 424

Lip-Reading *by Edward Nitchie*   ISBN: *1-59462-206-X*   **$25.95**
Edward B. Nitchie, founder of the New York School for the Hard of Hearing, now the Nitchie School of Lip-Reading, Inc, wrote "LIP-READING Principles and Practice". The development and perfecting of this meritorious work on lip-reading was an undertaking...   How-to Pages 400

A Handbook of Suggestive Therapeutics, Applied Hypnotism, Psychic Science   ISBN: *1-59462-214-0*   **$24.95**
by Henry Munro   Health/New Age/Health/Self-help Pages 376

A Doll's House: and Two Other Plays *by Henrik Ibsen*   ISBN: *1-59462-112-8*   **$19.95**
Henrik Ibsen created this classic when in revolutionary 1848 Rome. Introducing some striking concepts in playwriting for the realist genre, this play has been studied the world over.   Fiction/Classics/Plays 308

The Light of Asia *by sir Edwin Arnold*   ISBN: *1-59462-204-3*   **$13.95**
In this poetic masterpiece, Edwin Arnold describes the life and teachings of Buddha. The man who was to become known as Buddha to the world was born as Prince Gautama of India but he rejected the worldly riches and abandoned the reigns of power when...   Religion/History/Biographies Pages 170

The Complete Works of Guy de Maupassant *by Guy de Maupassant*   ISBN: *1-59462-157-8*   **$16.95**
"For days and days, nights and nights, I had dreamed of that first kiss which was to consecrate our engagement, and I knew not on what spot I should put my lips..."   Fiction/Classics Pages 240

The Art of Cross-Examination *by Francis L. Wellman*   ISBN: *1-59462-309-0*   **$26.95**
Written by a renowned trial lawyer, Wellman imparts his experience and uses case studies to explain how to use psychology to extract desired information through questioning.   How-to/Science/Reference Pages 408

Answered or Unanswered? *by Louisa Vaughan*   ISBN: *1-59462-248-5*   **$10.95**
Miracles of Faith in China   Religion Pages 112

The Edinburgh Lectures on Mental Science (1909) *by Thomas*   ISBN: *1-59462-008-3*   **$11.95**
This book contains the substance of a course of lectures recently given by the writer in the Queen Street Hail, Edinburgh. Its purpose is to indicate the Natural Principles governing the relation between Mental Action and Material Conditions...   New Age/Psychology Pages 148

Ayesha *by H. Rider Haggard*   ISBN: *1-59462-301-5*   **$24.95**
Verily and indeed it is the unexpected that happens! Probably if there was one person upon the earth from whom the Editor of this, and of a certain previous history, did not expect to hear again...   Classics Pages 380

Ayala's Angel *by Anthony Trollope*   ISBN: *1-59462-352-X*   **$29.95**
The two girls were both pretty, but Lucy who was twenty-one who supposed to be simple and comparatively unattractive, whereas Ayala was credited, as her Bombwhat romantic name might show, with poetic charm and a taste for romance. Ayala when her father died was nineteen...   Fiction Pages 484

The American Commonwealth *by James Bryce*   ISBN: *1-59462-286-2*   **$34.45**
An interpretation of American democratic political theory. It examines political mechanics and society from the perspective of Scotsman James Bryce   Politics Pages 572

Stories of the Pilgrims *by Margaret P. Pumphrey*   ISBN: *1-59462-116-0*   **$17.95**
This book explores pilgrims religious oppression in England as well as their escape to Holland and eventual crossing to America on the Mayflower, and their early days in New England...   History Pages 268

QTY

The Fasting Cure by *Sinclair Upton* ISBN: *1-59462-222-1* **$13.95**

In the Cosmopolitan Magazine for May, 1910, and in the Contemporary Review (London) for April, 1910, I published an article dealing with my experiences in fasting. I have written a great many magazine articles, but never one which attracted so much attention... New Age/Self Help/Health Pages 164

Hebrew Astrology by *Sepharial* ISBN: *1-59462-308-2* **$13.45**

In these days of advanced thinking it is a matter of common observation that we have left many of the old landmarks behind and that we are now pressing forward to greater heights and to a wider horizon than that which represented the mind-content of our progenitors... Astrology Pages 144

Thought Vibration or The Law of Attraction in the Thought World ISBN: *1-59462-127-6* **$12.95**

by *William Walker Atkinson* *Psychology/Religion Pages 144*

Optimism by *Helen Keller* ISBN: *1-59462-108-X* **$15.95**

Helen Keller was blind, deaf, and mute since 19 months old, yet famously learned how to overcome these handicaps, communicate with the world, and spread her lectures promoting optimism. An inspiring read for everyone... Biographies/Inspirational Pages 84

Sara Crewe by *Frances Burnett* ISBN: *1-59462-360-0* **$9.45**

In the first place, Miss Minchin lived in London. Her home was a large, dull, tall one, in a large, dull square, where all the houses were alike, and all the sparrows were alike, and where all the door-knockers made the same heavy sound... Childrens/Classic Pages 88

The Autobiography of Benjamin Franklin by *Benjamin Franklin* ISBN: *1-59462-135-7* **$24.95**

The Autobiography of Benjamin Franklin has probably been more extensively read than any other American historical work, and no other book of its kind has had such ups and downs of fortune. Franklin lived for many years in England, where he was agent... Biographies/History Pages 332

Name	
Email	
Telephone	
Address	
City, State ZIP	

☐ **Credit Card** ☐ **Check / Money Order**

Credit Card Number	
Expiration Date	
Signature	

Please Mail to: Book Jungle
PO Box 2226
Champaign, IL 61825
or Fax to: *630-214-0564*

ORDERING INFORMATION

web: *www.bookjungle.com*
email: *sales@bookjungle.com*
fax: *630-214-0564*
mail: *Book Jungle PO Box 2226 Champaign, IL 61825*
or PayPal *to sales@bookjungle.com*

Please contact us for bulk discounts

DIRECT-ORDER TERMS

**20% Discount if You Order
Two or More Books**
Free Domestic Shipping!
Accepted: Master Card, Visa,
Discover, American Express